Torrent!

by

Bernard Ashley

Illustrated by Roy Petrie

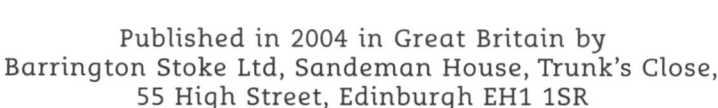

Published in 2004 in Great Britain by
Barrington Stoke Ltd, Sandeman House, Trunk's Close,
55 High Street, Edinburgh EH1 1SR

ISBN 1-842991-96-5

Printed in Great Britain by Bell & Bain Ltd

Barrington Stoke gratefully acknowledges support from the
Scottish Arts Council towards the publication of the
gr8reads series

Scottish
Arts Council
LOTTERY FUNDED

A Note from the Author

It was in all the papers and on TV. There was a flash flood in France. Water and mud came rushing down a river valley and swept away a holiday campsite. Many people died.

The year before, when the snows melted in a valley up in the Alps, a much bigger flood had killed a lot more people.

For this book, I put these two ideas together, the campsite and the Alpine flood. Then I read a news story about a man who had been given a lift on a motorbike and saved ... by someone who didn't stay to be thanked ...

For John and Wendy

Contents

Chapter 1
A Swim in the Dam

Tom was a fool to swim alone, but he'd got very hot on the long hike up the mountain – and the clear water of the Blue Dam looked so cool.

He tore off his clothes and dived in – and in a second he went from much too hot to ice-cold. Melting snow was running into the dam and the water gave him a crushing pain as the air was sucked out of his lungs. He had to get back to the side. He had to swim, or die.

Kick your legs! he told himself. *Work your arms! Get to the bank before you freeze to death!* And with his body blue he kept on swimming – till, just as everything went black, he grabbed at the bank. Somehow he had made it.

He pulled himself out and looked back at the dam. The water was rising, higher and higher. The dam was so full that even the flowers on the bank were under the water now. He took some photos of them. He was shaking so much it was hard to hold the camera still.

What a fool! He was lucky to be alive.

Back in his one-man tent down at the campsite, Tom looked at his photos. The flowers he'd seen under the water were called violas – "Drowned Violas".

But how had he saved himself from drowning? In the water he'd been hit by cramp – and you can't swim with cramp. Was it magic?

Chapter 2
Run for your Life!

"Get out!"

"Run!"

"The dam's giving way!"

The sun was up. It was morning and people were yelling outside Tom's tent. They were running past and falling over his tent pegs. What the hell was going on? Tom's head was still filled with a dream he'd had – he was swimming in the Blue Lake. He was with someone else – but who?

Loud shouts shook him awake – and when he poked his head out of the tent, the campsite was almost bare. People were rushing for the gate – on bikes and motorbikes, in cars and camper vans. They were racing to get away.

He saw the mountain stream across the
field. It ran down from the Blue Dam. But
it wasn't a stream any more, it was a river
– much wider now and spilling out across
the grass. Clumps of grass, bits of wood
and even small trees were rushing down in
the water.

"Come on! Run for it!" someone yelled.
"Get on the lorry!"

Tom looked over to the gate of the
campsite. The sheep farmer who ran the
site had backed his lorry out of the barn

and was about to go. The lorry was packed with the campers who didn't have cars or bikes.

"Come on!" People were yelling at Tom as the lorry started off. Tom ran for it. The dam was giving way and the river was rushing onto the site. When the dam broke the water would become a torrent. It would carry rocks and trees down with it and would wash away everything in the valley. Anyone or anything in its way would be swept to their death. So Tom had to get to that lorry in time.

But as he ran, still half-asleep with his dream, he tripped over his own tent peg. When he got up, the lorry was pulling away. It revved off down the road before he could get to it.

He was left there – alone with the rushing water that roared as it rose higher and higher. The road ran 2 miles down the mountain to the gap at the bottom of the valley. It went between high rocks on either side. At the bottom of the valley there was a bridge over the river.

If he couldn't get to the bridge before the rushing water swept it away he would be dead. But how could he run 2 miles in time?

Tom was going to die. He had almost died in the Blue Dam. Now he would drown in that same water as it came rushing down. It was the end for him – but he had to *try* to save himself. He mustn't give up!

He began to run down the road. He ran as he had never run before, his legs and arms pumping.

The water was over the campsite now and running beside him. The sound of it roaring down the mountain was getting louder – and there were small rocks in the racing water, jumping about like tennis balls. Soon there would be much bigger rocks. And it was no good getting up a tree. Uprooted trees were rushing past him all the time.

What was he going to do? He'd lost
hope.

Chapter 3
The Girl on the Moto

But what was that other sound? What could he hear as well as the noise of the raging water? It sounded like a moto.

And it *was* a moto – coming down the road from the campsite. A girl was riding

one of those small motorbikes, not much

bigger than a pushbike.

She must have been like me, asleep in her tent, Tom thought. He hadn't seen her in the campsite before, but she looked like someone he knew. She rode up to him, and stopped.

"Get on, boy! Quick!" She was French, pretty, wearing jeans.

"Thank you! Thank you!" Tom got onto the small seat behind her. It was only a bit longer than a seat for one.

"Hold on tight!" she said.

17

So he held the girl tight round the waist as she revved the moto and they bumped off over the grass.

But not down the road. She was going towards the trees.

"Where are you going?" Tom yelled.

"Road's no good! River washes it away! There's a track!"

"Are you sure?" he asked. They seemed to be riding into thick forest.

"I know this track! You come or not?"

"I come!" This moto was his only hope.
And he knew that she was right – the road
would soon be swept away by the torrent of
water. This other way could be their best
hope. They had to take a short cut. They
had to get down to the bridge before it was
swept away.

They raced into the trees. Tom had to
hang on to the girl as they bumped along a
small track. Twigs hit his face and stinging
nettles brushed his bare legs. He shut his

eyes and put his head down. He couldn't
see where they were going – but he had to
trust the girl. And for a few moments Tom
almost enjoyed hugging this girl tight as
they twisted their way down the mountain.

She took them into the trees. She had to
lean this way and that to keep on the track.
Tom held onto her. Where her body went,
he went with it. She knew the track so well,
she must have ridden it many times.

All at once, the girl looked back. She yelled a rude word in French. She had heard the same sound that Tom had just heard.

Help! What was that, racing behind them?

Chapter 4
Race for the Gap!

It was water. Roaring water. It was a
new river that was taking the same track
as they were. The same short cut! Tom
could hear it behind them, crashing through
bushes, bending trees.

"Water! Behind us!" he yelled.

"I know! I hear! Just hold on harder!"

And the girl did a sudden skid. She rode the moto uphill for a bit and shot along the side of the mountain. Now they were away from the track and riding through bushes and nettles. They twisted and turned and almost smashed into trees. Downhill again with leaves and twigs hitting them even harder. Tom could only just hold on.
He hugged the girl so tightly that they were like one person.

It worked! The new river didn't follow them – it stayed with the track – as they shot out into the open. But Tom's heart raced when he saw where they were. His head went light. No! Help! They couldn't do this!

They were at the top of a long, steep slope. They started to race down it – like the long drop of a big dipper! They were racing head first down the mountain. Bushes and rocks were in the way – one slip and they would be smashed.

The girl twisted and turned the handlebars as they raced down. Tom clung on tight and went with her, this way and that. He could feel his heart thumping against her back, his life in her hands.

It was so exciting that Tom didn't care any more about the danger. He yelled, "Yeah!"

If they crashed, they crashed.

He could hear the new river raging among the trees – as well as the roar of the main torrent as it swept down the road on a wide bend.

And it *was* a race! They had to make it to the bridge before it was swept away.

And they had to make it on the bike without crashing!

It jumped about, it bucked, it skidded – but the girl held on – and all at once they saw below them, at the end of the valley, the huge rocks on both sides of the gap. Now they could see the last bit of the road leading to the bridge. The bridge was still there, still standing. But for how long? The mountain had become a torrent of water.

Could they get there in time? They had to! If not they would die.

Chapter 5
Just!

The girl raced for the last bit of road
like a jockey or a bike champ.

The roar got much louder. The dam had
broken up. It was as if the side of the
mountain was falling down the valley.
It was going to smash the bridge.

As the girl skidded the moto onto the
road, the tarmac began to shake under
them. It was cracking. But there, in front
of them, was the bridge. People were
running over it, getting away.

Tom had held the girl tight all the way
down. Now, for extra speed, he reached
forward over her, put his hands down over
her hands on the grips and willed the moto
to race faster.

The moto shook on the cracking road – but with two pairs of hands Tom and the girl held it firm, racing for the bridge.

Behind them the torrent roared with a sound like the end of the world. The rocks loomed over them on both sides, forcing the water higher, faster, like a killer wave. In seconds the bridge would be smashed to bits and swept away.

But now their moto was on the bridge – which was shaking under them.

20 yards, 15 yards, 10 yards – would they get over the bridge in time? The shaking had become a rocking. They could only just hang on as the raging waters started to win, coming up over the bridge.

5 yards to go! If water got into the engine it would pack up and they would be swept away in seconds.

But with Tom reaching over and the girl gripping the handlebars hard, they made it to the other side. Just.

She twisted the moto hard to the left, and it shot up a side track onto higher ground, just as the great wave of water hit the bridge and swept it away.

The torrent rushed on. Trees, rocks, fences and bits of barn twisted and jumped in the racing water. There were tents and dead sheep and a car in the angry river.

The moto went up the track to high ground. People were all over the gardens of a big house. Here, Tom and the girl came off the moto and dropped down onto the

dry grass.

Chapter 6
Viola

Tom shut his eyes - but not to sleep. How could he sleep after an escape like that? He shut his eyes and thanked God that he was still alive.

He thanked God, and the girl. What a hero she was!

He opened his eyes. He rolled over to
thank her, to shake her hand, to kiss her.
He would like to kiss her.

But she wasn't there. The moto was
lying on the grass, but where was the girl?
He looked around, everywhere. People had
rugs round them. They were drinking mugs
of hot coffee. Some were crying with shock.
Others were looking for friends from the
campsite and the farms. But the girl wasn't
there.

He started to ask everyone – but they all told him the same thing. The same scary thing.

She had never been there. No-one had seen her. Tom had ridden into the garden on his own.

On his own? Did they think he was a fool? Was this some sort of bad dream? He didn't even know how to *ride* a moto!

But the more he told them about the girl, the more they shook their heads sadly.

He was in shock! The poor boy had been so scared he couldn't remember what he'd done. They were so sure that he'd ridden into the garden on his own that he almost started to think it must be true.

Until the sheep farmer from the campsite saw the moto.

"Who took this?" he yelled in French. "Who stole my girl's moto?"

People pointed at Tom. The farmer came over to him. *He's going to hit me,*

Tom thought. But he didn't. He spoke in English.

"Thank you," he said. "You saved her moto from the barn. And the barn is ..." He was close to tears. "... smashed and swept away – with my campsite."

"No," said Tom. "*She* saved the moto. And she saved me."

But the farmer looked at him with an angry face.

"That is not funny!" he said. "Do not make jokes!"

"It's not a joke," Tom told him. "It's true. She rode up to me and told me to get on the back ..."

The farmer's hands dropped to his sides. He looked Tom in the eye. "And how could she do that?" he said. "She is dead. 5 years, she is dead. I keep her moto. She loved it. It is all I have left of her ..."

Tom stared back. He had gone cold. Colder than in the Blue Dam. He could hardly ask what he wanted to ask.

"How did she die?" But he knew what he was going to be told.

"In the Blue Dam," the farmer said. "She swam alone, it was too cold, and she died ..."

Tom almost sank to the ground. His legs felt weak. Now he knew who it was in his dream. He knew who had helped him swim back to the bank of the dam ... where the drowned flowers grew.

The girl. The dead girl.

Tom looked into the farmer's eyes.

"And what was her name?" he said softly.

"Viola," the farmer said. "My girl was Viola."

Again Tom had known what he would be told.

Drowned Viola of the Blue Dam.

Barrington Stoke would like to thank all its readers for commenting on the manuscript before publication and in particular:

Lewis Antoniou
Nick Bate
Josh Beavon
Jamie Berry
Oliver Biddle
Emma Bovill
Simon Brown
Matthew Burke
Mrs J Casson
Helen Dodds
M. Edmundson
Jonathan Flynn
Dan Green
John Griffin
Bradley Griffiths

Kelly Hume
Daniel Keane
Philip McInerney
Siobhan Moffat
Julia Naden
Leanne Oakley
Scott Parrott
Anne Pearce
Dara Rice
Ryan Russell
K. Simpson
Paul Steele
Sean Talbot
Dominic Warrican
David Young

Become a Consultant!

Would you like to give us feedback on our titles before they are published? Contact us at the address below – we'd love to hear from you!

Barrington Stoke, Sandeman House, Trunk's Close,
55 High Street, Edinburgh EH1 1SR
Tel: 0131 557 2020 Fax: 0131 557 6060
E-mail: info@barringtonstoke.co.uk
Website: www.barringtonstoke.co.uk

If you loved this book, why don't you read ...
Luck
by
Alison Prince
ISBN 1-842991-99-X

NO LUCK 4 DALE!

Dale hates school. He has no luck with girls. He fights with his mum. So how did he get to be a hero?

You can order *Luck* directly from our website at
www.barringtonstoke.co.uk

If you loved this book, why don't you read ...
Coma
by
David Belbin
ISBN 1-842991-97-3

GIRLFRIEND IN A COMA

A crash in the dark. Todd's girlfriend Lucy is in a coma. And now Todd's started seeing Jade. But what if Lucy wakes up ...?

You can order *Coma* directly from our website at
www.barringtonstoke.co.uk

If you loved this book, why don't you read …
The Beast
by
Michaela Morgan
ISBN 1-842991-98-1

BEAST IN THE WOODS

Oooooooooooooooo! Was it the wind in the trees? Was it a ghost? Or was It … could it be … a BEAST?

You can order *The Beast* directly from our website at **www.barringtonstoke.co.uk**